PLAYDATE PALS

PUPPY
LEARNS TO SAY
PLEASE

Rosie Greening • Dawn Machell

make
believe
ideas

One day **Puppy** and his friends were making pictures together.

Puppy was creating
a big, starry scene!

Puppy had chosen his stars and he wanted to stick them down.

He looked around, but Hippo had the glue.

"Hippo, give me the glue!" said **Puppy**.

Puppy had forgotten to say **please**!

"That's **rude**!" thought Hippo,
and she moved to another table.

Then **Puppy** decided to put glitter on his stars.

But Kitten was using the glitter.

Puppy said, "Kitten, I want the glitter!"
and **grabbed** it from her.
Puppy had forgotten to say **please**!

"That's not very **kind**," said Kitten, and she went to join Hippo.

Soon, **Puppy** had finished his picture.

He wanted to hang it on the wall,
but he couldn't reach.

"Someone help me!" yelled **Puppy**.
Puppy had forgotten to say **please**!

Kitten said, "We don't feel like helping you. You took the glue and the glitter without saying **please**!"

That made **Puppy** feel **sad**.

Puppy was **sorry** that he had forgotten to use such an important word.

He wanted to make it up to his friends,
so he helped them finish their pictures.

Kitten and Hippo smiled and said,
"Thank you, **Puppy**!"

When all the pictures were finished,
Hippo brought in some sandwiches.

Puppy wanted a sandwich,
and he knew what he needed to say.

"**Please** may I have a sandwich, Hippo?"
asked **Puppy**.

Puppy had remembered to say **please**!
Hippo grinned and gave him a sandwich.

"**Thank you**," said **Puppy**. He smiled at his friends – he was happy he had said **please**!

READING TOGETHER

Playdate Pals have been written for parents, caregivers, and teachers to share with young children who are beginning to explore the feelings they have about themselves and the world around them.

Each story is intended as a springboard to emotional discovery and can be used to gently promote further discussion around the feeling or behavioral topic featured in the book.

Puppy Learns to Say Please is designed to help children learn about the importance of saying please when expressing their wishes. Once you have read the story together, go back and talk about any experiences the children might share with Puppy. Talk to children about saying please and then encourage them to do so in other trusted relationships.

Look at the pictures

Talk about the characters. Do they look happy when Puppy doesn't say please? What about when he does say please? Help children think about how saying please affects others.

Words in bold

Throughout each story there are words highlighted in bold type. These words specify either the **character's name** or useful words and phrases relating to **saying please.** You may wish to put emphasis on these words or use them as reminders for parts of the story you can return to and discuss.

Questions you can ask

To prompt further exploration of this behavioral topic, you could try asking children some of the following questions:

- When should you say please?
- How do you feel when people don't say please?
- If you want a piece of fruit, how should you ask for it?
- What is good about saying please?